The Art Lesson

Written and illustrated by

Tomie dePaola

PAPERSTAR

The Putnam & Grosset Group

For ROSE MULLIGAN,
my fifth grade teacher,
who ALWAYS gave me more
than one piece of paper…
…and, of course,
BEULAH BOWERS, the best
art teacher any child
could have had.

Also, special thanks to
Binney & Smith Inc.
and Crayola crayons. —TdeP

published in 199 by The Putnam & Grosset Group, 345 Hudson Street,
New York, NY 10014. PaperStar is a registered trademark of
The Putnam Berkley Group, Inc. The PaperStar logo is a trademark of
The Putnam Berkley Group, Inc. Originally published in 1978
by G. P. Putnam's Sons. Published simultaneously in Canada.
Manufactured in China
Crayola is a registered trademark of Binney & Smith Inc. Used with permission.

Library of Congress Cataloging-in-Publication Data
dePaola, Tomie. the art lesson/written and illustrated by Tomie de Paola. p. cm..
Summary: Having learned to be creative in drawing pictures at home,
young Tommy is dismayed when he goes to school
and finds the art lesson there much more regimented.
[1. Artists–Fiction   2. Individuality–Fiction.] I. Title.
PZ7.D439Ar 1989[E]–dc19 88-27617 CIP AC
ISBN 0-698-11572-4
30 29 28 27 26 25 24

Tommy knew he wanted to be an artist when he grew up.
He drew pictures everywhere he went. It was his favorite thing to do.

His friends had favorite things to do, too. Jack collected all kinds of turtles. Herbie made huge cities in his sandbox. Jeannie, Tommy's best friend, could do cartwheels and stand on her head.

But Tommy drew and drew and drew.

His twin cousins, who were already grown up, were in art school learning to be real artists. They told him not to copy and to practice, practice, practice. So, he did.

Tommy put his pictures up on the walls of his half of the bedroom.

His mom put them up all around the house.

His dad took them to the barber shop where he worked.

Tom and Nana, Tommy's Irish grandfather and grandmother, had his pictures in their grocery store.

Nana-Fall-River, his Italian grandmother, put one in a special frame on the table next to the photograph of Aunt Clo in her wedding dress.

Once Tommy took a flashlight and a pencil under the covers and drew pictures on his sheets. But when his mom changed the sheets on Monday and found them, she said, "No more drawing on the sheets, Tommy."

His mom and dad were having a new house built, so Tommy
drew pictures of what it would look like when it was finished.

When the walls were up, one of the carpenters gave Tommy
a piece of bright blue chalk.

Tommy took the chalk and drew beautiful pictures all over the
unfinished walls.

But, when the painters came, his dad said, "That's it, Tommy.
No more drawing on the walls."

Tommy couldn't wait to go to kindergarten. His brother, Joe, told him there was a real art teacher who came to the school to give ART LESSONS!

"When do we have our art lessons?" Tommy asked the kindergarten teacher.

"Oh, you won't have your art lessons until next year," said Miss Bird. "But, we *are* going to paint pictures tomorrow."

It wasn't much fun.

The paint was awful and the paper got all wrinkly. Miss Bird made the paint by pouring different colored powders into different jars and mixing them with water. The paint didn't stick to the paper very well and it cracked.

If it was windy when Tommy carried his picture home, the paint blew right off the paper.

"At least you get more than one piece of paper in kindergarten," his brother, Joe, said. "When the art teacher comes, you only get one piece."

Tommy knew that the art teacher came to the school every
other Wednesday. He could tell she was an artist because she
wore a blue smock over her dress and she always carried a big
box of thick colored chalks.

Once, Tommy and Jeannie looked at the drawings that were hung up in the hallway. They were done by the first graders.

"Your pictures are much better," Jeannie told Tommy. "Next year when we have real art lessons, you'll be the best one!"

Tommy could hardly wait. He practiced all summer. Then, on his birthday, which was right after school began, his mom and dad gave him a box of sixty-four Crayola crayons. Regular boxes of crayons had red, orange, yellow, green, blue, violet, brown and black. This box had so many other colors: blue-violet, turquoise, red-orange, pink and even gold, silver and copper.

"Class," said Miss Landers, the first-grade teacher, "next month, the art teacher will come to our room, so on Monday instead of Singing, we will practice using our crayons."

On Monday, Tommy brought his sixty-four crayons to school. Miss Landers was not pleased.

"Everyone must use the same crayons," she said. "SCHOOL CRAYONS!"

School crayons had only the same old eight colors.

As Miss Landers passed them out to the class, she said, "These crayons are school property, so do not break them, peel off the paper, or wear down the points."

"How am I supposed to practice being an artist with SCHOOL CRAYONS?" Tommy asked Jack and Herbie.

"That's enough, Tommy," Miss Landers said. "And I want you to take those birthday crayons home with you and leave them there."

And Joe was right. They only got ONE piece of paper.

Finally, the day of the art lesson came. Tommy could hardly sleep that night.

The next morning, he hid the box of sixty-four crayons under his sweater and went off to school. He was ready!

The classroom door opened and in walked the art teacher. Miss Landers said, "Class, this is Mrs. Bowers, the art teacher. Patty, who is our paper monitor this week, will give out one piece of paper to each of you. And remember, don't ruin it because it is the only piece you'll get. Now, pay attention to Mrs. Bowers."

"Class," Mrs. Bowers began, "because Thanksgiving is not too far away, we will learn to draw a Pilgrim man, a Pilgrim woman and a turkey. Watch carefully and copy me."

Copy? COPY? Tommy knew that *real* artists didn't copy.
This was terrible. This was supposed to be a real art lesson.
He folded his arms and just sat there.

"Now what's the matter?" Miss Landers asked. Tommy looked
past her and spoke right to Mrs. Bowers.

"I'm going to be an artist when I grow up and my cousins told
me that real artists don't copy. And besides, Miss Landers won't
let me use my own sixty-four Crayola crayons."

"Well, well," Mrs. Bowers said. "What are we going to do?"
She turned to Miss Landers and they whispered together. Miss
Landers nodded.

"Now, Tommy," Mrs. Bowers said. "It wouldn't be fair to let
you do something different from the rest of the class.

But, I have an idea. If you draw the Pilgrim man and woman and the turkey, and if there's any time left, I'll give you *another* piece of paper and you can do your own picture with your own crayons. Can you do that?"

"I'll try," Tommy said, with a big smile.

And he did.

And he did.

And he still does.